# Rascal: A Meowmoir

Written by Claire Noble
Illustrated by Brigitte Noble

Claire Noble
P.O. Box 4039
Edwards, CO 81632
www.clairenoble.org

Publisher's Note: This is a work of fiction. Names, characters, places, and incidents are a product of the author's imagination. Locales and public names are sometimes used for atmospheric purposes. Any resemblance to actual people, living or dead, or to businesses, companies, events, institutions, or locales is completely coincidental.

Book design © 2013, BookDesignTemplates.com

Ordering Information: Special discounts are available on quantity purchases by corporations, associations, and others. For details, contact the publisher at the address above.

Claire Noble and Brigitte Noble — First Edition

ISBN 978-1495483134

Printed in the United States of America

For all of our furry family members,
past and present,
Miao Mao, Hei Mao, Spicy and Rascal

Rascal's mom was wild. Not pizzas for breakfast or loud rock 'n' roll on the radio wild, but wild because she lived on her own and not with a family. Sadly, she was sick when she gave birth to Rascal. Because of her illness, Rascal's eyes were damaged and he was born blind. His first home was under a tree in the countryside outside of the large, busy city of Hong Kong.

Special rescuers who look for wild cats found Rascal and took him to an animal doctor called a veterinarian. The vet gave Rascal a checkup and discovered that except for his eyes, Rascal was a healthy kitten. Rascal was placed with a foster family who took care of him until a forever home could be found for him. The rescuers put a photo of Rascal online so people searching for a pet to adopt could see how cute he looked.

One day, Mrs. Noble searched online for a kitten to be a friend for Hei Mao, the Noble family cat. Hei Mao was from Shanghai, China, and he was very proper and formal. He was mostly black with little patches of white that made him look like he was wearing a tuxedo. Mrs. Noble thought Hei Mao seemed lonely ever since the family moved from Shanghai to Hong Kong. Another cat, she decided, would keep him company. She also wanted the Noble children, Brigitte and Kendall, to learn how to care for a kitten, since Hei Mao was already an adult cat when they were born.

When Mrs. Noble saw the picture of Rascal, she knew he was the one. Mr. Noble was worried about taking care of a blind cat, but Mrs. Noble convinced him they could do it. She contacted the cat rescue and asked to adopt Rascal.

Rascal's foster mom put him in a basket and took a red Hong Kong taxi to the Noble family's apartment. Rascal was very scared when he arrived at his new home. At first, Hei Mao was not very nice to Rascal. Mostly he ignored Rascal, but sometimes he hissed at him. Everyone called Hei Mao the grumpy uncle.

Soon Rascal relaxed and explored every corner of the apartment. He could not see, but he could hear and smell. Also, his whiskers helped him navigate and let him know when he was getting close to walls and furniture. Sometimes he moved too fast and bumped his head. If he did not have a hard head before, he had one now. He liked to sneak up and pounce on Hei Mao. Everyone except Hei Mao thought that was funny.

Once, Rascal was allowed outside on the balcony. He hesitated at first, poking his nose outside and feeling the breeze on his whiskers. He slowly explored the balcony, sniffing as he walked along the glass railing. Then, he slipped through a narrow gap in the railing onto a tiny ledge, forty-three stories above the ground. Mrs. Noble was worried that Rascal was going to fall. Then, Rascal slipped back through the narrow gap from the ledge to the balcony, as if it was no big deal. Mrs. Noble never allowed Rascal on the balcony again.

Rascal was two years old when the family prepared to move from Hong Kong to Switzerland. Before they left Hong Kong, they moved to a temporary apartment that did not allow pets. Rascal and Hei Mao had to stay at a special pet hotel. Rascal did not understand that he was only staying in the pet hotel a few months. He thought it was forever. That made him sad, and his sadness made him sick. Rascal must have had a broken heart, because the vet could not find anything medically wrong with him.

However, when it was time to leave for Switzerland, the vet did not want Rascal to get on the airplane. He thought Rascal was too sick to fly, but the Noble family would not leave Rascal in Hong Kong. At the airport, Rascal and Hei Mao were put in travel containers called crates, along with a small amount of food and water. Then their crates were loaded into a special compartment on the airplane. The Noble family was excited about moving to Switzerland, but they were worried about Rascal.

**When** the Noble family arrived in Switzerland, Rascal would not eat or drink. He was very skinny. He could no longer walk. Mrs. Noble found a Swiss vet near their new home and took Rascal to him. The vet told the family that Rascal's condition was very serious. Rascal needed to go to the animal hospital right away.

**Mrs. Noble,** Kendall and Brigitte put Rascal in the car and drove to Zurich to find the animal hospital. The doctors at the hospital said they would try to help Rascal, but they did not think he would make it.

To everyone's surprise, Rascal's condition improved. In just a few days he was feeling much better. The Noble family was relieved to see he was finally eating and drinking a little. They were told they could take him home. Rascal needed medicine every day. Day-by-day, he got stronger and healthier. Two weeks after leaving the hospital, Rascal walked outside in the garden of his new home in Switzerland. This was the first time since he was rescued in Hong Kong as a kitten that Rascal had been outside.

Then Rascal disappeared. Days passed and the family wondered where he could be. "Where was he sleeping?" Brigitte asked. "What was he eating?" Kendall wondered. Rascal was in danger. He had no idea what cars and trucks were, or that they could hurt him if he got in their way. Rascal did not even know what a dog was. The Noble family wondered if they would ever see Rascal again.

**Mr. Noble,** Kendall and Brigitte put up signs around the neighborhood with Rascal's picture on it. The signs asked people to call if they saw Rascal. No one called.

Then, a week after he wandered away, Rascal came walking back into the garden. He looked fine. He was not hurt but he was hungry. If the Noble family could speak cat, Rascal would have told them where he went.

Even though Rascal was not hurt, he seemed to have learned his lesson and never wandered too far from home again. At his home in Switzerland he has a warm bed inside and plenty of yummy food and cool water. His Aunt Brenda sends him homemade catnip treats. A small door allows him to go outside in the garden when he wants to get some fresh air.

Like many other cats, Rascal likes to hunt, but hunting is difficult for a blind cat. He tried to hunt birds, but they just teased him. Rascal discovered that he could hunt things that are noisy, like bees. When he catches a bee, he eats it. Sometimes when he is feeling generous, he brings a bee to Mr. Noble, who pretends to eat it.

When the weather is fine, Rascal likes to sit outside in the sun. He sits in the middle of the garden with his nose twitching and his ears pointing straight up.

**Hei Mao** is still grumpy, but on cold days he and Rascal curl up together to stay warm.

Rascal still pounces on Hei Mao, and Hei Mao still does not think it is funny.

CPSIA information can be obtained
at www.ICGtesting.com
Printed in the USA
LVIC05n0312011214
416392LV00017B/58